SPOOKY SLEUTHS

Read them all . . . if you dare.

The Ghost Tree
Beware the Moonlight!

SPOOKY SLEUTHS 2

Beware the Moonlight!

Natasha Deen

illustrated by Lissy Marlin

A STEPPING STONE BOOK™
Random House 🏠 New York

Text copyright © 2022 by Natasha Deen
Cover art and interior illustrations copyright © 2022 by Lissy Marlin

All rights reserved. Published in the United States by Random House Children's Books, a division of Penguin Random House LLC, New York.

Random House and the colophon are registered trademarks and A Stepping Stone Book and the colophon are trademarks of Penguin Random House LLC.

Visit us on the Web!
rhcbooks.com

Educators and librarians, for a variety of teaching tools, visit us at
RHTeachersLibrarians.com

Library of Congress Cataloging-in-Publication Data
Names: Deen, Natasha, author. | Marlin, Lissy, illustrator.
Title: Beware the moonlight / Natasha Deen; illustrated by Lissy Marlin.
Description: First edition. | New York: Random House Children's Books, [2022] | Series: Spooky sleuths; 2 | "A Stepping Stone book." | Audience: Ages 6–9. | Summary: Asim and his friends realize that the astrophysicist helping teach their class about the moon is actually a Moon-Gazer intent on brainwashing the entire town.
Identifiers: LCCN 2022003790 (print) | LCCN 2022003791 (ebook) | ISBN 978-0-593-48890-4 (trade) | ISBN 978-0-593-48891-1 (lib. bdg.) | ISBN 978-0-593-48892-8 (ebook)
Subjects: CYAC: Supernatural—Fiction. | Folklore—Guyana—Fiction. | LCGFT: Novels.
Classification: LCC PZ7.1.D446 Be 2022 (print) | LCC PZ7.1.D446 (ebook) | DDC [Fic]—dc23

Printed in the United States of America
10 9 8 7 6 5 4 3 2 1

This book has been officially leveled by using the F&P Text Level Gradient™ Leveling System.

Random House Children's Books supports the First Amendment and celebrates the right to read.

Penguin Random House LLC supports copyright. Copyright fuels creativity, encourages diverse voices, promotes free speech, and creates a vibrant culture. Thank you for buying an authorized edition of this book and for complying with copyright laws by not reproducing, scanning, or distributing any part in any form without permission. You are supporting writers and allowing Penguin Random House to publish books for every reader.

For my parents —N.D.

*To my family. Thank you for
your support. —L.M.*

1

I hurried through the Saturday afternoon mist to meet my group for our science assignment. Lion's Gate, Washington, was always foggy. One of my friends, Rokshar Kaya, said it was because the town was on an island surrounded by ocean and mountains. Another friend, Max Rogers, thought it was because Lion's Gate was full of supernatural creatures.

I agreed with Max. My family had moved here a month ago, and it was the creepiest place we'd ever lived! I rushed past one of the scarier spots in town, the row of abandoned houses. With their broken windows and missing doors, the homes looked like skulls, ready to devour anyone who came too close.

The wind rattled the branches of the dead trees and blew away the mist. I stumbled to a stop. Someone was in one of the houses, walking by the window.

Impossible, I thought. *The houses are off-limits to everyone.* Movement flashed again. Whatever was up there, it was going too fast to be human.

No way was I staying here! The fog rolled in, and I ran as hard as I could before the thing spotted me. My sneakers slapped the pavement. Once I was clear of the houses, I stopped to catch my breath.

Then, from behind, I heard it. A soft

wailing sound. The hair on the back of my neck rose as I turned. A shadowy blob was coming toward me. The creature grew bigger and louder as it drew closer.

The creature came out of the mist.

It was Rokshar and Max!

"You scared me!" I said. "I thought you were a monster!"

"I was showing Rokshar the wood pan-pipe my uncle Nelson got me," Max said.

He blew on it.

I winced.

So did he. "I need to practice more."

"Ready to work on our assignment?" asked Rokshar.

Max put away the pipe, and we walked to Rokshar's house. When we got there, we went to her room.

Max sat on Rokshar's bed and pulled out a sheet of paper. Our teacher, Mx. Hudson, had given the class a set of challenge questions to work on over the weekend. They said it was a hint about our upcoming science unit. The group that put in the best effort for the unit would win a pizza lunch. My friends and I were determined to be that group!

"Give examples of electromagnetic radiation and list their sources," Max said. His mouth fell open. "What is that?"

"It's the scientific term for *light*," said Rokshar.

"Oh," he said, relieved. "Sunlight, and the source is the sun." He wrote that down.

"What about ultraviolet light?" I asked.

"That comes from the sun, too," said Rokshar. "Another source of it is a SAD lamp."

Max frowned. "How can a lamp be sad?"

Rokshar laughed. "No. It's an acronym. It's a lamp for people who have seasonal affective disorder—*S-A-D*, SAD," she said. "The lamp emits ultraviolet light. It mimics sunlight and helps some people feel better."

Max wrote it down.

We added radio waves, microwaves, X-rays, and infrared light to our list.

"Next question," said Max. "What can you make out of plastic bottles, a cork, tape, air, and water?"

That stumped everyone but Rokshar. "They can be used to make bottle rockets."

"Last one," said Max. "What is Duchess's favorite treat?"

Duchess was a bearded dragon and our class mascot.

"Even easier," said Rokshar. "Seedless watermelons."

Once we finished the assignment, I told them about seeing someone—or something—in the houses.

"Why did you tell me?" Max flopped back on the bed. "I'm having a hard enough time sleeping after the haunted tree."

A few weeks ago, we'd discovered a ghost tree in the old cemetery. It had taken control of our teacher and Max's uncle. My friends and I had saved them—with the help of Rokshar's older brothers.

The adults didn't know the truth.

I was okay with that. Mom and Dad would ground me until forever if they thought I'd taken on a supernatural bad guy.

"I still think it was a lab experiment that went wild," said Rokshar. "But we don't have evidence."

I didn't need proof. I had my gut instinct. But Rokshar wanted to be a

scientist, and she was all about gathering evidence.

"I have proof," said Max. He pushed up his sleeve and held out his arm. "When the hairs go up, creepy things are happening. I bet something weird is going on in the empty houses."

"It might have just been the reflection of tree branches off the windowpane," Rokshar said.

Maybe, but my gut said something terrifying was about to happen in Lion's Gate.

2

"Let's go!" I said to my folks. "We're wasting moonlight."

Mx. Hudson's questions about light and bottle rockets had me thinking about the moon. If my group included a photo of it, that might show our effort. And if I added a cool fact—that moonlight was really the moon's surface reflecting sunlight—maybe we'd win the pizza lunch.

We got to a spot on the hill that Dad said was one of the best places to get an awesome photo. Below us, Lion's Gate was lit up in a grid of streetlights, shops, and houses. On our right was the forest.

"I have lots of moon photos." Dad grunted as he set up the telescope. "You could use one of mine." Dad was an astrophysicist at Eden Lab, and Mom worked there as a marine biologist.

"I want to take a great photo, not borrow yours," I said.

"It's too bad your assignment is due on Monday," he said. "The full moon will be out in a few days. That would have made for the ultimate shot."

I looked at the sky. "It would have been cool to get a photo of the moon with some stars surrounding it."

"Outdoor lights, like streetlights, can block starlight," said Dad. "It's called light pollution."

"There's light pollution in Lion's Gate?" I asked. "We're the only town on the island." That was because almost everyone worked for the lab—a top research facility with secret projects—including Rokshar's and Max's parents.

"Even in a town as small as ours," said Dad, "light pollution can cause problems."

Mom took out her phone and lifted it skyward. "I was going to show you a light pollution map, but I can't get cell service."

"That'll change once the town is finished building the cell towers and laying the cables for Wi-Fi," said Dad.

"It'll be nice to have better coverage," said Mom, "but I'm sorry it means losing the old cemetery." She elbowed me in the ribs. "Where will the ghosts live then?"

Like me, Mom loved spooky stuff. Unlike me, she thought they were just stories. I knew supernatural creatures were real, and I was okay if the ghosts had to leave town!

"Somewhere sunny," said Dad. "I hear rain dampens their spirits."

We groaned at his dad joke.

I went to the telescope to look at the moon. Only, something white and shining caught my attention. "There are lights moving in the forest."

"I've heard about that," Dad said. "People at the lab say it always happens around the time of the full moon."

"Maybe it has to do with natural electric magnetic pulses, like the sun's plasma or lightning." Mom wiggled her eyebrows. "Or maybe it's vampires or werewolves."

"Be serious," I said, pretending the idea of vampires living in the forest wasn't going to give me nightmares.

I peered through the eyepiece, looking for the unusual lights. Instead, I saw the round, white surface of the moon. I watched as it rose over the treetops. But then, what I'd thought was the moon spun around. I was looking at a giant set of eyes and a forehead! I yelped and stumbled backward. Then I checked again. Something big and bright and taller than the trees was walking through the forest! "There's a face in the treetops!"

"What!" Dad leaped to the equipment. "Someone's trapped in a tree?"

"No—" I gulped for air. "There's a giant in the forest!" *With a pair of angry eyes that stared at me.* I shuddered at the memory.

There was silence. Then my parents laughed.

"You almost had me," said Dad. "A giant in the forest!"

"No! Really—" I pointed at the treetops, but the lights had disappeared.

"Maybe it was the man in the moon," said Mom. "He's heard you're taking photos of his home, and he doesn't like it."

"I saw something!" I said.

Dad patted me on the shoulder. "Let's see." He checked the forest. So did Mom.

"I'm sorry, sweetie," she said. "We don't see anything."

"I'm not joking," I said, trying not to tremble.

"I don't think you are, either," said Dad. "But it's late and you're tired. Let's head back. You can use one of my photos of the moon."

I argued, but it was no use. They were determined to send me to bed. I trudged home. A giant with a glowing face was in the forest. Something creepy was definitely going on in Lion's Gate, and I was going to find out what it was.

3

On Monday, I walked with my friends to school and told them what I saw in the forest.

"I'm sure the lab is behind it," Rokshar said. "This is our chance to prove their experiments sometimes run wild."

"Or we prove the supernatural is real," I said.

"How are we going to do that?" asked Max.

"This weekend," Rokshar said, tapping

her chin, "we'll go to the forest and look for evidence."

Max frowned. "That sounds like it could be dangerous."

"We'll be careful," said Rokshar. "My brothers, Devlin and Malachi, will keep us safe."

"Do you think Asim saw a giant?" asked Max.

Rokshar shook her head. "A person who's tall enough to be a giant would be too heavy to survive."

When we got to the classroom, Mx. Hudson was bouncing with excitement. I sat at my desk. Rokshar sat across from me. Max was behind her.

After Mx. Hudson took attendance, they asked us to turn in our assignment. "Any guesses on what we're studying?"

"Light!" said Elijah from the back row.

"Try again," said Mx. Hudson.

"Watermelons?" asked Sydney.

Mx. Hudson shook their head.

I thought about light, radiation, and bottle rockets. "Is it space?"

"Close!" said Mx. Hudson. "We'll be studying the moon. I have a special surprise to help us."

I gave myself a mental high five. Adding a photo of the moon to our assignment was sure to win us the pizza lunch!

There was a knock at the door. A tall, pale man dressed in a white suit stepped inside. His icy-blue eyes met mine. A shiver ran down my spine. I whispered to my friends, "He gives me the creeps."

"Shh," said Rokshar. "Don't be mean."

"I'm with Asim." Max slid the sleeve

of his sweater up. "Goose bumps. Nothing good happens when I get goose bumps."

"This is Mr. Maan. He's an astrophysicist at the lab," said Mx. Hudson. "His studies take him out of town a lot, but he returned this weekend. When he heard about our moon study, he couldn't wait to come and talk to us about it."

"I'm thrilled to be here," droned Mr. Maan.

"Thrilled?" Sydney whispered. "Why does he look so grouchy?"

Mx. Hudson shushed her, but I agreed. Mr. Maan didn't seem very happy to be with us.

He turned his cold gaze on us. "Who can tell me a fact about the moon?"

"It has craters and no atmosphere," Max said.

Mr. Maan winced. "Please lower your voice."

I blinked. Max hadn't been that loud.

Mr. Maan turned to Rokshar. He smiled at her, but it looked like he was baring his teeth.

Rokshar shrank into her seat.

"Do you know something interesting about the moon?" he asked her.

"It helps Earth regulate its climate," she said.

"Do you think we might live on the moon one day?" Elijah asked Mr. Maan.

"Traveling to the moon isn't for everyone. Neither is studying it," said Mr. Maan. "Perhaps we should do something else."

Mx. Hudson laughed as though he had made a joke, but I thought, *He doesn't like the idea of us studying the moon.* That didn't make sense. Shouldn't he be excited about our unit? I looked away before he caught me staring.

My brain spun. Lights and a glowing giant in the forest, and the sudden appearance of Mr. Maan. What did it all mean?

After school, I went to my room and took out my journal. Rokshar and I were keeping records of the creepy things we were

investigating. We'd agreed to use the scientific method. I started writing.

Step One, my question.

> I saw lights in the forest and a glowing
> giant. Are these two things linked to a
> supernatural cause?

Step Two was the hypothesis. But I
didn't have one yet. My gut said Mr. Maan
was connected to the strange goings-on,
but I didn't know how.

Gathering evidence was Step Three,
and I knew where to start.

4

As I helped with dinner, I told Dad about my day and asked him about Mr. Maan.

"I haven't met him," said Dad. "I've heard he's totally into studying the moon." He grinned. "They say he's over the moon about his job."

I groaned. "Be serious. Mx. Hudson says Mr. Maan travels a lot. You're an astrophysicist, too, but you don't travel."

"He and I study different things," Dad said. He stirred the rice. "If you still want to take some photos, there's a clearing

in the forest. Apparently, it's Mr. Maan's favorite spot. Some people say he comes back every full moon just for the view, so we know it'll be great."

The memory of Mr. Maan's scowling face rose in my mind. I didn't believe it was a coincidence that he showed up right after creepy things started happening. After dinner, I went to my room and added a time line in my journal.

Saturday
Night: A light and a glowing giant appeared above the treetops. Also, Mr. Maan returned to town.

Monday
Morning: Mr. Maan's at school to help with our moon study, but he doesn't like the idea of people going to the moon. (Plus, he seems sensitive to sound.) These light- and giant-sightings only began after he returned to town.

I tapped my pencil and thought. Mr. Maan wasn't tall enough to be a giant, but if he was supernatural, maybe he could change his size. But why would a giant live in Lion's Gate? I wrote everything down, including Mom's ideas about plasma and her jokes about vampires and werewolves. Now that I had a hypothesis about Mr. Maan being supernatural, I needed proof.

After my parents went to bed, I snuck into the office, where I could see the forest. I perched by the window seat and watched, hoping I'd see something that would help me solve the puzzle.

The next morning, I met up with Rokshar, Max, Devlin, and Malachi. We headed to school. As we walked down the hill toward the old graveyard, I told them about Dad's idea for a moon photo. "Do you want to come?"

"For sure," said Malachi, brushing his

dreads off his face. "Something spooky is definitely happening." He nodded at the gates of the cemetery. "Maybe like last time, with the ghost tree."

Max shivered. "I'm glad it's gone."

"Maybe not," said Malachi. He pointed. On the other side of the gate, a light was moving through the mist. It was white, tall, and thin.

My body felt hollow. "That's like what I saw in the forest, except it was bigger."

"Maybe it's someone with a flashlight," said Rokshar. "Let's find out."

After making sure no construction people were around, we crept inside the cemetery. The wind swept between the leafless trees and gravestones, and made a chilling, moaning cry. I stepped carefully around the weeds.

"There," whispered Rokshar, squinting through the fog. The light was floating to the center of the graveyard.

We sped up. The mist and wind dulled the noise of our sneakers.

I hoped they dulled the thundering of my heartbeat, too.

Suddenly, Malachi slammed to a stop. He stuck out his arm to bring us to a halt. Putting his index finger to his mouth, he whispered, "Do you hear that?"

Pop! Pop! Pop! It sounded like fire-crackers going off.

"Stay here," said Devlin. "Malachi and I will look."

"Not likely," muttered Rokshar, and she took the lead. We snuck closer, but the mist made it hard to see.

I squinted, but I couldn't tell if it was a person with a light or a light all by itself. It moved around the safety cones marking the holes where the Wi-Fi cables were being laid. The light disappeared into a hole, and the popping sound started again.

"They're messing with the Wi-Fi cables," said Malachi.

The light—or person—climbed out of the hole and sped away from us. We followed, but as we ran closer to the hole, there was a hiss and a pop. Sparks erupted from the ground. We leaped away as the grass caught on fire.

"Hey! You! Stop!" someone—an adult—yelled.

We whirled around. The yelling faded into the distance.

"They must be chasing after the person," said Devlin. "Let's get out of here!"

"We can't just leave—there's a fire!" said Rokshar.

Malachi cupped his hands around his mouth. In his deepest voice, he boomed, "Fire! Fire!"

There was silence, then, "Fire! Fire!" Other adults took up the cry. We waited until we heard footsteps coming our way.

"Over here!" Malachi yelled at them. He turned to us. "Let's go!"

We raced out of the cemetery before anyone knew we were there.

5

When we got to school, Mx. Hudson was feeding Duchess. "Change of plans for today," they said. "Our Wi-Fi is down. Someone vandalized the cables in the cemetery and around town."

"That's terrible!" I said, pretending to be surprised. "Why would anyone do that?"

Mx. Hudson sighed. "Some people like the remoteness of our town. Look at Mr. Maan. He travels a lot, but when he comes back, all he wants to do is spend time in the forest."

Just then, Mr. Maan came into the room. "The principal told me about the vandalism," he said, trying to hide his smile. "How horrible."

I have to add him being happy about the vandalism to my journal, I thought.

He brushed his sleeve and dirt fell.

Dirt? Like from being in the cemetery? I wondered.

Mr. Maan walked away, and I stared at him. Yesterday, he'd been tall and pale. Today, he seemed taller, brighter . . . just like the light in the cemetery. I leaned toward my friends. "Is he glowing?" I whispered.

"It's his white clothing," Rokshar whispered back. "It's reflecting the light."

She was the smartest person I knew. Maybe she was right about Mr. Maan. Maybe he was grouchy because of the noise. And maybe his suit was reflecting the classroom lights. Or maybe he was a supernatural creature, and he was gaining power because the full moon was near. I raised my hand and said, "Mr. Maan, you seemed unhappy when we talked about traveling to the moon—"

"I don't blame him," said Mx. Hudson as they put a photo of the moon on the whiteboard. "Until we learn how to care for Earth, we shouldn't be leaving it."

I looked at Mr. Maan to see if he agreed, but he wasn't listening. He was staring at the photo. His body seemed to go fuzzy and soft. Mr. Maan's eyes turned white and began to shimmer.

I froze. Before I could nudge Rokshar or Max, I blinked, and he returned to normal. Had I imagined it, or had Mr. Maan transformed when he looked at the moon?

"He might have an eye condition that makes it seem like his eyes turn white in certain light," said Rokshar.

It was after school. Rokshar had invited Max and me over for dinner. We were eating cookies for dessert in her kitchen and talking about what I had seen.

"Have you heard of anything like that?" asked Devlin.

"No," she admitted, "but there's lots I don't know."

Malachi poked her. "You know everything."

She grinned and nudged him back.

"It's not an eye condition," I said. "It's proof that Mr. Maan is a supernatural creature. His body definitely got blurry. And he glows, just like the light at the cemetery. I bet he's the giant—I bet he can make himself taller or shorter if he wants."

"How do we get evidence that Mr. Maan isn't human?" asked Malachi.

"In some TV shows," I said, "the alien's blood is a different color. Maybe supernatural creatures are similar."

Rokshar shook her head. "Humans can have blood conditions that make their skin look blue."

"My granddad has diabetes, and one time, it made his breath smell really sweet," said Max. "Would something like that be proof?"

"Do you want to get close to Mr. Maan and smell his breath?" asked Malachi.

Max shuddered. "No."

"Sweat," I said. "Maybe there's something in his sweat."

"Seriously," Devlin groaned. "Stop."

Rokshar thought about it. "We need to go to the forest this weekend and look for clues."

After school on Wednesday, I walked home alone. I stopped, pulled out my journal, and added what I'd learned.

* There was a light in the cemetery, and someone ripped up the Wi-Fi cables. Mr. Maan was happy about this.

* Some people (like Mr. Maan) want Lion's Gate to stay remote.

* Was he the light we saw at the cemetery?

I closed my book. Mr. Maan had turned gooey when he saw the moon. I put that together with Dad's talk about light pollution. Could it be that Mr. Maan was here because Lion's Gate had the best view of the moon?

No, that didn't make sense. The moon could be seen from any place on Earth. Still . . . I couldn't shake the feeling Mr. Maan, the moon, the light, and the vandalism were connected. I put away my book.

Just then, I saw Mr. Maan walking down the street. I followed him to the row of vacant houses, then scrambled behind a row of dead bushes and hid, hoping he wouldn't spot me. He strode to the front door of the middle house. Even in the gloomy afternoon light, he seemed to shine. Mr. Maan looked over his shoulder and scanned the street.

I crouched down even lower.

He stared straight at the bushes and squinted.

I held my breath, didn't blink, and didn't move.

He went inside. I dashed after him. I crept along the porch and hid below a window. I peeked inside. Mr. Maan was crossing the room toward the fireplace.

The board under me creaked.

He spun around, and I ducked under the windowsill.

A few seconds later, I heard a low hum. Light spilled from the window. When I peeked inside again, Mr. Maan had disappeared.

6

The next afternoon, my friends and I went to the library to do some research. We split up and searched the books for answers. I didn't find anything, so I wandered around the library.

"Any luck?" I asked Max when I saw him.

"I read about leaf sheep," he said. "They're ocean slugs that use algae to photosynthesize." He rubbed his head. "Researching light can take you down some wild paths. Did you find anything?"

I sighed. "No." I turned and noticed a familiar figure at one of the library computers. "Max," I whispered. "Look!"

It was Mr. Maan. He was hunched over a computer screen.

"Can you see what he's looking at?" I asked.

Max craned his head. "No."

"Me either. Come on!" I pulled him behind one of the bookshelves. We hid and watched Mr. Maan. As soon as he got up, I raced to the computer. Excellent! He hadn't cleared his browser history. I scanned the links.

So did Max. "Mirrors?" He frowned.

"Why would anyone be looking at mirrors?"

"That's my business, isn't it?" Mr. Maan's voice sounded behind us.

I spun around and gulped at the scowl on his face. "Oh—ah— Is this your computer? Sorry, we were just going to look up some things."

Mr. Maan squinted at us, then stepped close. "Are you spying on me?"

"Asim, Max, what are you doing here?" Mx. Hudson appeared behind Mr. Maan. Rokshar, Malachi, and Devlin were with them.

I sighed in relief. "Extra research for our moon project. The full moon's tomorrow, and we want to do something amazing."

Mx. Hudson grinned. "Us too! We're going to—"

Mr. Maan put his hand on the teacher's shoulder.

I heard a soft hum, just like back at the house. The spot under Mr. Maan's hand began to glow. "It's a surprise," he said in a soft voice.

Mx. Hudson's eyes glazed over. "It's a surprise," they repeated in a monotone.

Mr. Maan bared his teeth in a fake smile.

I stumbled back. So did everyone else.

"I suppose we can tell you," he said. "We're no longer studying the moon. We are going to study watermelons instead. Isn't that correct?"

Mx. Hudson, their eyes still unfocused, nodded. "Watermelons."

Mr. Maan released his grip. "We'll see you later." He and Mx. Hudson left.

"Okay, I know I wasn't the only one who saw that!" I said.

"Super weird!" said Devlin.

"Did he—did he just take away our moon study?" sputtered Rokshar.

"Uh-oh," said Malachi. "No one gets in between Rokshar and science."

"That was proof he's supernatural," said Devlin. "No one can glow."

"He wasn't glowing," said Rokshar. "It was the suit."

"I'm confused," said Max. "Isn't Mr. Maan an astrophysicist? Why would he want to stop us from studying the moon? And why does he wear clothes that light up?"

"I think I know!" said Rokshar. "He's working on a light suit. Remember what I said about the SAD lamps? Light can affect our moods. I think Mr. Maan's figured out a way to use light to influence people's thoughts and actions." Her expression turned grim. "That's dangerous. He got Mx. Hudson to stop our moon study. What else can he make our teacher do?" She slung her bag over her shoulder. "We need to stop Mr. Maan before it's too late."

I thought about Mx. Hudson and worried it was already too late.

7

When I got home, I went to my room. I pulled out the notebooks Mom and I had filled with supernatural myths.

"There has to be an answer here," I told myself.

Mom tapped on my door. "Want some hot chocolate?"

"Yes, please!" I said. "Do you know any supernatural creatures that glow and love the moon?"

"Not personally," she said. "But I'm sure they're lovely."

"Be serious," I groaned.

She sat with me. "Werewolves, vampires, and some types of witches love the moon, but I don't think they glow."

"That's what I thought, too," I said. I tried to sound casual as I asked, "Have you met Mr. Maan?"

She peered at me. "What is your fascination with him? I heard you asking your dad about him the other day."

"What? Nothing—" I almost told her about Mr. Maan making Mx. Hudson stop our moon study, but I didn't know how to explain it. "He's just . . . not nice to us kids."

Mom sighed. "I'm sorry, honey. Not every adult likes children, but I'm sure he's been a great resource for your moon study."

"It's weird that he showed up at the same time as the lights in the forest," I said. "And he's not helpful with the moon study at all."

Mom chuckled. "With a name like his, you'd think he'd be excited to help with the study."

"His name?" I repeated.

"Maan," Mom said. "It's Dutch for *moon*."

Moon. Glowing lights. A giant. A bolt of realization zipped through my body. I knew what Mr. Maan really was, and I'd been right all along. Something terrifying was going to happen in Lion's Gate.

"A Moon-Gazer?" Malachi's face wrinkled. "What's that?"

My friends and I were walking to school. "A Moon-Gazer is an incredibly tall, thin man. He can be forty feet or even a hundred feet tall," I said. "And he comes from the Caribbean. People say he's in love with the moon. He straddles the roads and watches it. If you disturb him while he's moon-gazing, he crushes you between his legs."

"I'm too young to be crushed!" Max squeaked.

"Or he squeezes you to death, like an anaconda," I said.

Max's face paled.

"Killing you just because you interrupted his looking at the moon?" said Devlin. "That's harsh."

"One of the stories says his family lives on the moon. Some say he attacks people so they won't see his family and try to capture them," I said.

"But Mr. Maan isn't gigantically tall," said Rokshar.

"Maybe not in his human form," I said.

"How do we stop him?" asked Malachi.

"That's the problem," I said. "There's no answer. All the stories say to avoid him or run really fast."

Devlin groaned. "That's the worst advice."

"He's not a Moon-Gazer," said Rokshar. "He's a human being with dangerous technology."

"He's a Moon-Gazer." I patted my bag. "And I have a way to prove it."

When we got to the school doors, I put my plan in action. I'd borrowed some of Dad's moon photos. "Mr. Maan will go gooey when he sees them," I said to Rokshar and Max. "You'll believe me when his body turns blurry and liquid."

We went into the classroom. Mr. Maan was by Duchess's cage. This morning, he seemed even brighter than before.

"My dad's an astrophysicist," I told him. "He likes the moon, too. Do you want to see some of his pictures?"

"No," said Mr. Maan, "because we're no longer studying the moon."

"They're great photos," said Max. "You'll love them."

"They're very detailed," added Rokshar.

Mr. Maan came closer and he seemed to glide with every step.

My mouth went dry, and I clutched the photos to my chest.

His frigid gaze swept over each of us. My fingers tingled as he took another step toward us, but I didn't move.

"Why do you care so much about me seeing these pictures?" he asked.

He was so close, I had to crane my head back to see his face. Mr. Maan leaned into me.

"Do you know something I don't?" he asked softly.

My legs did their overcooked noodle impression. "Only that the moon is amazing," I said, and heard my voice tremble.

Mx. Hudson came into the room.

Rokshar took the photos from me. "You said we weren't going to study the moon anymore," she said to Mx. Hudson. "But take a look at these incredible photos. Won't you please change your mind?"

Mx. Hudson reached for the pictures, but Mr. Maan was faster. He put his hand on our teacher's shoulder. "The unit is finished," he murmured, light just visible under his hand.

Mx. Hudson's eyes went dull. "The unit is finished."

"But—" Rokshar said.

"Don't push it or you'll fail the unit," said Mr. Maan, sneering in her direction.

Mx. Hudson repeated Mr. Maan's words.

"What about the pizza lunch for the winners?" asked Max.

"There is no pizza lunch for anyone," said Mr. Maan.

"There is no pizza lunch for anyone," droned Mx. Hudson.

Mr. Maan smirked. "Now that the study is finished, I don't need to be here anymore."

I had to stop him before he crushed someone between his legs. Pushing down my fear, I chased after him. "Where are you going?" I asked.

"For a walk."

"In the forest?" I pressed.

He watched me for a minute. Then he smiled as if I was amusing. "Tonight, I'll be back at the forest."

That smile made me mad. Just because I was a kid, he thought I couldn't stop any terrible plans he had for Lion's Gate. The

story about the Moon-Gazer's family living on the moon tickled my brain. I stood tall and asked, "The forest? What about your family? Don't you want to spend time with them?"

"I do," he said. "We love to meet in the forest." His snarky smile returned. "It's much quieter there, now that the Wi-Fi and cell tower construction is delayed. No more interfering technology." He left.

Mx. Hudson blinked, then shuffled to their desk.

Max's face grew stormy. "Did he make Mx. Hudson take away our pizza lunch? No one gets to steal our pizza!"

"Focus," Rokshar said to him. "The point is, he's controlling Mx. Hudson somehow."

"But—" Max started to say.

"There's no way Eden Lab would let anyone work on a project that could mess with a person's mind like that." Rokshar's voice shook with anger. "Asim, we have to put our plan in place. We're going to need your dad's help. Will you see if he'll take us to the forest?"

I nodded.

"Tonight," she said, "we stop Mr. Maan."

"This is great," said Dad as my friends and I climbed off our bikes. "I've been hoping to get some photos of the moon from the forest."

Our plan was to find evidence that Mr. Maan was either a Moon-Gazer or a scientist with an unauthorized experiment. But Dad couldn't know that. So I'd told him we wanted photos of the moon for our science unit.

I spotted Mr. Maan heading into the

forest. "Dad, is the strap for the telescope secure?"

Dad bent to check it and didn't see Mr. Maan. Perfect. We were going to follow Mr. Maan, but if Dad knew that, he'd never allow it.

"We should head out," Devlin said to my dad. He pointed at the spot where Mr. Maan had gone. "Maybe that way?"

"The hill with the best view of the moon is just ahead," said Dad, checking the directions on his phone.

We walked a little farther, when I heard it. The humming. My pulse sped up.

"That's odd," Dad said, confused. "There shouldn't be any sounds like—"

Just then, a familiar glow lit up the trees in front of us.

"Stay here," said Dad. He moved

forward. The trees hid him from view.

"He shouldn't be alone," I said to my friends. "Mr. Maan is dangerous." My body felt like dough, but I took a step. "Come on."

As we hurried to the hill, we heard a loud, deep roar. The sound went through me. I slapped my hands over my ears and fell on my knees. The roar came again. Light flashed. There was a bang. Leaves and chunks of bark exploded around us.

Dad raced into view. "Run!" he screamed. "Run!"

We turned and sped for safety as the forest blew up behind us.

My legs churned and my lungs burned, but I kept running. Two beams of light appeared on either side of me. The humming made my eardrums vibrate. The lights closed in on me. Fast. Their brightness made my eyeballs throb. I threw myself on the ground and rolled. The lights collided behind me with an earsplitting *crack*. Pieces of trees rained down.

I stumbled to my feet. Everyone was in front of me, running hard. Dad must have seen me fall because he was rushing

to help me. The lights were on either side of him. They closed in, just like they had with me.

I screamed for him to duck, but he couldn't hear me. I sprinted for him, pointing at the lights. Dad kept running my way. Just as the lights scissored over him, Malachi tackled him from behind. They slammed into the ground. The lights blasted the trees around them. With a final roar, the lights disappeared into the darkness.

They faded as Dad and Malachi got to their feet. Our group raced for the end of the forest. Soon, we were out in the open again. Nothing came out of the trees. I collapsed on the ground, breathing hard.

"What was that?" Devlin panted.

The Moon-Gazer, trying to smash us between his legs. I glanced at Max and could tell he was thinking the same thing.

"I don't know," said Dad, gulping for air. "I got into the clearing. There were two vertical lights—I think they were lasers. Someone aimed them in my direction, and suddenly trees were exploding!" Dad paced away, then swung back. "Do you know how dangerous that was? No one is allowed to use lasers in the forest!

I'm taking you kids home. Then I'm going to the lab and reporting it! Let's go!"

Dad dropped us at our house. While he explained to Mom what had happened, Rokshar and Max called their parents.

"Dad." I stopped him as he was putting on his coat. "Mr. Maan was in the forest tonight."

Dad's face went slack. "You think he was trapped by the lasers?"

I took a deep breath. "I think he was the one using them."

"He was ahead of us, Mr. MacInroy," Rokshar said. "If he had been attacked, he would have run in our direction. You would have seen him."

Dad's expression grew troubled. "Thank you," he said. "I'll tell everyone at the lab." He kissed Mom and left.

When Mrs. Kaya and Ms. Rogers arrived, Mom made everyone snacks while we waited for Dad to return.

"Is the lab working with lasers?" Rokshar asked her mom.

"The scientists work with lots of things," she said. "But messing around with lasers is extremely dangerous. No scientist would risk their job by doing something like this." Mrs. Kaya hugged each of us. "I'm so relieved everyone is okay!"

When Dad returned, we rushed to find out what had happened.

"They're sending in a team to investigate," said Dad, taking off his coat.

"Until then, the forest is off-limits to everyone."

"What did they say about Mr. Maan?" asked Max.

Dad's eyes glazed over. "Mr. Maan wasn't involved," he said in a robotic tone. "We made a mistake. He wasn't in the forest."

My blood turned to ice. Mr. Maan had gotten to my dad.

9

We had to figure out a way to get our parents to let us return to the forest. The next day, everyone came to my house. We were in the kitchen with Dad when Mom found us.

"Did you hear that Mr. Maan is leaving town tonight?" she asked.

"So soon?" asked Dad.

"It's for his work," said Mom, "but it's too bad. I would have liked a chance to meet him."

"I'm sure he'll be back," said Dad.

My friends and I glanced at each other. That's exactly what we were afraid of.

"Whatever bad thing he's planning, it's happening tonight, when the moon is full," I whispered to them.

Malachi agreed.

My parents' phones beeped.

"Is everything okay?" I asked as they read their texts.

"No," Mom said, her voice tightening with worry. "There's been a break-in at the lab."

That had to be Mr. Maan!

"Was anything taken?" Rokshar asked.

"I'm not sure," said Dad.

"There's already been trouble at the cemetery and lasers in the forest," said Mom. "What if someone broke into the lab to vandalize people's work?" She frowned at the phone screen. "I have some specimens growing, and they're delicate."

I glanced at Malachi and Devlin. This was our chance!

"You should go," said Malachi. "Devlin and I can watch everyone."

Mom and Dad made eye contact.

I held my breath and tried to make it look like I wasn't holding my breath.

"If you're sure—" Mom started to say.

"So sure! Get going!" said Devlin.

As soon as they left, I ran to my room and brought back my journal. "If we're going to stop Mr. Maan, we have to figure out what he's doing."

Rokshar pulled out her journal. We hovered over the books, reading and rereading.

The puzzle pieces crowded my brain. If

the stories about the Moon-Gazer's family living on the moon were correct, that would explain why Mr. Maan was always staring at it. And why he came to Lion's Gate. Dad said the forest gave Mr. Maan the best view. But what was he planning?

"The mirrors!" cried Rokshar. "Mirrors reflect and amplify light. He can use them to make his suit more powerful. And with a powerful suit, he could make the entire

town do the same thing at the same time. There must be something at the lab he needs. That would explain the break-in."

"Like something that would help him permanently stop the Wi-Fi and cell tower construction," said Malachi. "Or worse."

"Max," I said, "we're going to need your panpipe."

"We'll also need pot lids, whistles," said Rokshar, "and a few other things."

We gathered everything we needed, then got on our bikes.

It was time to stop Mr. Maan.

"He should be here soon," I said. We tucked our bikes into the trees and waited.

Mr. Maan arrived, but he didn't see us. We followed him to the spot on the hill.

He turned his face to the full moon. His body began to shimmer and go liquid. He arched his back. His body grew brighter. He began to grow—taller and thinner.

I wanted to run and hide, but Mr. Maan had messed with my dad and my teacher. Even though I was terrified, I moved toward him. Rokshar pulled me back.

"We have to see where he put the mirrors," she whispered. "Wait until the light reflects off them."

Mr. Maan leaned back. A bright light beamed from his chest and went skyward, toward the moon. It looked like a bridge. He began to glow. One by one, mirrors placed near the trees began to light up. The circle grew brighter.

"Hit him with your flashlights!" I said.

We aimed them at him, but his light was so bright, ours did nothing.

"The mirrors!" said Rokshar. "Break the mirrors!"

"Won't that bring bad luck?" asked Malachi.

"A Moon-Gazer is building a bridge to the moon," said Devlin, hauling him away. "And he's going to brainwash the town. How much worse do you think our luck can get?"

While Devlin and Malachi ran to the mirrors, Max, Rokshar, and I sped to Mr. Maan. We yelled and called, but his eyes stayed closed. "He's in some kind of trance," I said.

Rokshar reached into her bag and handed me a mirror. "You have better

aim. If you throw it at the bridge, maybe it'll break the beam."

I hurled the mirror at the beam. It glinted, then glowed as it caught and reflected the light back to Mr. Maan. He grunted and stumbled back, but he didn't break his concentration.

Suddenly, the beam flickered and died. I glanced over my shoulder. Malachi and Devlin were sprinting to the mirrors, flipping them upside down.

Blinking, Mr. Maan looked around and saw us.

Mr. Maan growled. He bent down to swat at Rokshar. She leaped out of the way.

"Run for the trees!" yelled Devlin.

We bolted for cover and raced in different directions.

Behind me, I heard the branches crack

as Mr. Maan crashed through the forest. I jumped over roots and brambles. My breath came out fast and panicked. There was a bang, and chunks of bark hurtled toward me.

I glanced back and tripped over my feet.

"You!" he yelled. "I'm going to get you!"

I stumbled upright. Mr. Maan's cold hands locked around my ankles and yanked me off my feet. I kicked and yelled, but he hung on and dragged me to him.

The faint sound of sirens echoed in the air.

I kept kicking. "The forest is off-limits. Someone's seen your light," I panted, struggling to get free. "You're not getting away!"

"Yes, I am," he snarled. "But not before I'm done with you!"

Malachi and Devlin charged in from different directions and tackled him. He roared and blasted them off with his light. Mr. Maan gave me a sinister grin.

Suddenly, a piercing wail cut the night.

Mr. Maan winced and ducked his head. The sound came again. Mr. Maan let go of me and pressed his hands against his ears. "Stop it!"

Max ran into the clearing, his panpipe in his hands. He kept playing. Malachi and Devlin struggled to their feet.

Mr. Maan dropped to his knees and howled.

"Perfect! Keep going!" I yelled as Rokshar ran to us.

"Here!" She dumped out her bag. Pot lids, cymbals, and whistles fell to the ground. "His sensitivity to noise! We can use it against him!"

Each of us grabbed a whistle. Malachi, Rokshar, and Devlin banged the pot lids. I crashed the cymbals together. We blew the whistles.

"No! No!" Mr. Maan screamed. He hunched into a ball and pressed his hands against his ears. "Stop! Stop it!" He grew brighter and brighter.

Suddenly, he began to shake, harder and faster.

The air became staticky and dry and vibrated against my skin.

"He's going to blow! Let's get out of here!" yelled Malachi.

We ran.

The vibrations grew so intense, I felt them in my teeth. We raced for the forest's edge. A blinding cloud of light engulfed us. There was a terrible *BANG!* A shock wave blasted us off our feet.

I groaned and stood. My head was pounding. "Is he gone?"

Devlin pointed at a layer of white powder that dusted the ground and our clothes. "So much for the Moon-Gazer."

Vehicle lights flickered between the trees and the sirens' wails grew closer. "Let's get out of here!"

We shook off the dust and biked back to my house. My parents arrived a few minutes later.

"How was it?" Rokshar asked, and I envied how casual she sounded.

"All good." Mom squinted at me. "Did you go to the forest?"

"The forest? Why?" I hoped I sounded curious and not guilty.

"There were reports of the lasers again, as well as a large explosion," Mom said. "Are you sure you don't know anything about it?"

We shook our heads.

"One of the police officers who went into the forest said they saw a group of kids riding away on bikes soon after

people reported the lights and the explosion," Dad said, giving me a firm look.

"The forest is off-limits," I said. "We
know that."

Mom nodded. "Good. I'm happy to hear it."

After my parents left the room, I leaned into my friends and whispered, "Good thing they be*leafed* me, huh?"

My friends groaned.

I laughed.

Notes from Rokshar's Journal

- The question of Mr. Maan is a puzzle. While much of what he did fit Asim's hypothesis about Mr. Maan being a Moon-Gazer, his actions also fit my hypothesis that he was a rogue scientist with an unauthorized experiment.

- I have seen that he—or at least, his suit— was behind the lights in the forest. But I have no definitive proof that Mr. Maan, and not his suit, was responsible for influencing Mx. Hudson and Mr. MacInroy. There are many chemicals that can affect the human brain.

Suit glows

Why??
— Batteries?
— Paint?
— Chemicals?
— Reflective?

Battery powered?

- I also question Mr. Maan's ability to shift his shape. Holographic technology could make him appear to change, while glow-in-the-dark clothing would explain the glow.

- There are things I cannot explain. How did Mr. Maan disappear so suddenly on the night we confronted him? And why did he seem to have such a problem with noise?

- I'm left with no proof to support either a supernatural or a scientific cause.

- Conclusion: I cannot say with certainty that Mr. Maan was a Moon-Gazer.

Glow-in-the-dark paint?

Glow-in-the-dark thread?

Or fabric?

Notes from Asim's Journal

* I'm positive Mr. Maan was a Moon-Gazer, and I have proof.

* He showed up at the same time as the lights in the forest and the appearance of the giant.

* Mr. Maan went gooey when he looked at the moon. He could transform his appearance, and he gave off a light that had the power to control minds. A Moon-Gazer kills his victims by using his legs as weapons. The explosions in the forest involved two vertical beams of light. I know those were his legs.

Replace flashlight batteries

Beams of light = Moon-Gazer's legs?

Light = Mind control?

* Conclusion: My friends and I saved the town from a Moon-Gazer's invasion.

Author's Note

The Moon-Gazer story was one of the spookiest tales I heard growing up: A tall, thin man dressed in white, who stood astride the roads and looked at the moon. A man who, if disturbed, had no problem crushing you to death!

There were many variations of the story. Some said he was forty feet tall; some said he was a hundred feet tall. In some versions, his family lived on the moon. In another version, he was the only one of his kind. He was known to stand alongside roads, but there were also accounts of him wandering by the ocean's edge.

In every version, though, the creepiest part was that the Moon-Gazer could not be defeated. Run, hide, or avoid him altogether. This was all a person could hope to do.

As a writer, it was a lot of fun creating a way for Asim and his friends to defeat Mr. Maan, but their solution is a work of the imagination. Who knows how a person could really defeat a Moon-Gazer. If you ever encounter one, take my ancestors' advice and run the other way!

GET A SNEAK PEEK AT
THE NEXT BOOK IN THE
SPOOKY SLEUTHS SERIES.

Turn the page . . . if you dare!

I grabbed Max. "There's someone under the water!"

He looked over the railing. The woman scowled at us. Max called Rokshar over.

"Oh my gosh!" she said. "We should get Mx. Hudson before the seal leaves. I bet it's curious about our boat!"

Seal? Max and I peered over the railing. A small seal stared back at us.

"No," I told Rokshar. "It was a woman!"

"She had long brown hair," Max added.

My stomach churned. "She might be

that ghostly figure we saw floating on the beach last week."

"That's definitely a seal," said Rokshar.

"I'm sure it was a person," I said.

Max nodded.

"When light hits water, it bends. Maybe the refraction made the seal look like a woman." Rokshar tightened her purple ponytail. "Anyone swimming under-water would need breathing equipment. It would cover their nose and mouth."

"Maybe," I said, but I knew what I'd seen.

Rokshar and Max walked to the wheel-house. I gave the seal one last look. Behind it, a gigantic, bright green fish tail rose from the sea, slapped the waves, then dis-appeared into the water. The seal barked and swam away.

What kinds of fish are bright green, big,

and live in the Salish Sea? I couldn't think of any. Rokshar and I were keeping track of weird things that happened in Lion's Gate. We agreed to use the scientific method so our records were similar. A disappearing woman under the water and a mysterious fish needed recording!

Captain Hoxha slowed to our second stop. I wrote my observations in my journal.

- Last week, my friends and I saw a ghostly figure floating on the sand.
- Today, a woman was under the water and following our boat.

Step one of the scientific method was to ask a question.

- Why was she doing this? Is she connected to the ghostly figure?
- The only bright green fish I know live in tropical waters. Why is there a giant one in the Salish Sea?

I thought about what I'd seen and the stories Dad had told me about our Scottish heritage. I added my hypothesis, which was step two.

Selkies are sea people who can transform from seals into humans. My hypothesis is that the woman is a selkie.

As I was putting my journal back into my bag, there was a loud *bang,* and the boat tilted to one side. Some of my classmates screamed. Others slipped and fell on the deck. I slid but stayed on my feet. Fear made my mouth dry.

"Stay calm!" Mx. Hudson yelled. They stood on the other side of the boat from me. "Hold on to the railing and make your way to the wheelhouse!"

Another metallic *bang* rang out. The boat lurched. I slipped. My knees cracked against the ground.

"What's happening?" cried Sydney.

"Just a strong wave," said Mx. Hudson. "Calmly come to me!"

I hurried toward my teacher.

"Don't run, Asim," said Mx. Hudson.

I slowed down. There was a final, terrible crack as something hit us again. The boat tipped to the water's edge!

WANT MORE MYSTERY, SCIENCE, AND ADVENTURE?

Check out these chapter book series!

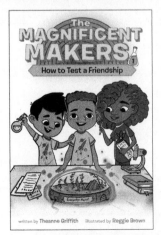

New friends. New adventures. Find a new series... just for you!

ISADORA MOON
For ballerina and fairy and vampire lovers

MAGIC ON THE MAP
For adventurers

UNICORN ACADEMY
For unicorn lovers

PUPPY PIRATES
For dog lovers

PuRRmaids
For mermaid and cat lovers

BALLPARK Mysteries
For sports fans

RHCB rhcbooks.com